Dear Parent:
Your child's love of reading starts here!

Every child learns to read in a different way and at his or her own speed. Some go back and forth between reading levels and read favorite books again and again. Others read through each level in order. You can help your young reader improve and become more confident by encouraging his or her own interests and abilities. From books your child reads with you to the first books he or she reads alone, there are I Can Read Books for every stage of reading:

SHARED READING
Basic language, word repetition, and whimsical illustrations, ideal for sharing with your emergent reader

BEGINNING READING
Short sentences, familiar words, and simple concepts for children eager to read on their own

READING WITH HELP
Engaging stories, longer sentences, and language play for developing readers

READING ALONE
Complex plots, challenging vocabulary, and high-interest topics for the independent reader

ADVANCED READING
Short paragraphs, chapters, and exciting themes for the perfect bridge to chapter books

I Can Read Books have introduced children to the joy of reading since 1957. Featuring award-winning authors and illustrators and a fabulous cast of beloved characters, I Can Read Books set the standard for beginning readers.

A lifetime of discovery begins with the magical words "I Can Read!"

*Visit www.icanread.com for information
on enriching your child's reading experience.*

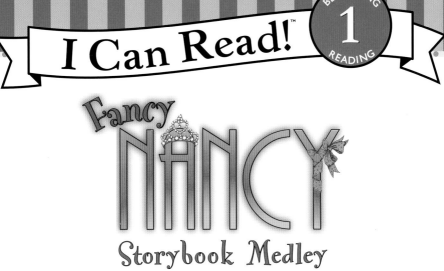

Fancy NANCY
Storybook Medley

by Jane O'Connor
pictures based on the art of Robin Preiss Glasser

HARPER
An Imprint of HarperCollins*Publishers*

I Can Read Book ® is a trademark of HarperCollins Publishers.

FANCY NANCY STORYBOOK MEDLEY

Fancy Nancy and the Boy from Paris
Text copyright © 2008 by Jane O'Connor
Illustrations copyright © 2008 by Robin Preiss Glasser

Fancy Nancy at the Museum
Text copyright © 2008 by Jane O'Connor
Illustrations copyright © 2008 by Robin Preiss Glasser

Fancy Nancy Sees Stars
Text copyright © 2008 by Jane O'Connor
Illustrations copyright © 2008 by Robin Preiss Glasser

Fancy Nancy: The Dazzling Book Report
Text copyright © 2009 by Jane O'Connor
Illustrations copyright © 2009 by Robin Preiss Glasser

Fancy Nancy: Pajama Day
Text copyright © 2009 by Jane O'Connor
Illustrations copyright © 2009 by Robin Preiss Glasser

Fancy Nancy: The Show Must Go On
Text copyright © 2009 by Jane O'Connor
Illustrations copyright © 2009 by Robin Preiss Glasser

ISBN 978-0-06-201213-5

10 11 12 13 14 LEO 10 9 8 7 6 5 4 3 2 1

Table of Contents

Fancy NANCY

Storybook Medley

I Can Read!

BEGINNING 1 READING

Fancy NANCY

and the Boy from Paris

by Jane O'Connor

cover illustration by Robin Preiss Glasser

interior illustrations by Ted Enik

HARPER

An Imprint of HarperCollins*Publishers*

I almost always get to school early.

But on Monday I am tardy.

(That's a fancy word for late.)

I come in and see a new kid.

He is standing next to Ms. Glass.

"Robert comes from Paris!"

Ms. Glass is telling everyone.

"He just moved here."

Paris!

Paris is a city in France.

It is gorgeous.

(That is a fancy word for beautiful.)

"Bonjour," I say in the book nook.

(In French that means "hello.")

"I am Nancy.

I never met anybody

from Paris before."

I speak slowly so he will understand.

"It's really nice there," Robert says.

"I miss it."

He has a book on cowboys.

He probably wants to learn

all about this country.

"I want to go there someday."

I show him my book.

It is about a dog in Paris.

"Do you like the United States?"

"Yes," says Robert. "Don't you?"

"Yes, I do," I say.

"I've lived here all my life."

Then Ms. Glass puts a finger
to her mouth.

"This is not talking time," she says.

"This is reading time."

On Tuesday

I sit next to Robert at lunch.

"Have you ever been

to the Eiffel Tower?"

I ask him.

Robert nods and swallows.

"Lots of times.

Our house was near it."

I tell Robert,

"I know about the Eiffel Tower.

There's a poster of it in my room.

I know lots about Paris."

I share some of my lunch.

"These are donut holes," I say.

Robert gives me a funny look.

"I know that.

I have eaten donut holes before."

That night

I tell my mom and dad about Robert.

"He is very nice.

He already speaks English.

I want to be his friend.

How do you say friend in French?"

"The word is *ami*," my mom says.

"You say it like this: ah-mee."

I love French.

Everything sounds so fancy!

"Why don't you ask him

over to play?" my dad says.

So the next day I do.

"We can play soccer.

Did you play soccer in Paris?"

"Sure. All the time," Robert says.

"I am a good kicker.

I can come on Friday."

On Thursday it is Show and Share.

Robert brings in a toy horse.

It is brown and white.

"My grandpa has a horse like this."

Then Robert passes around a photo.

"I miss her a lot.

Her name is Belle.

In French that means beautiful."

"Belle," I say to myself.

Now I know another French word.

On Friday Mom is at work.

Mrs. DeVine picks us up from school.

"Mrs. DeVine lives next door,"

I tell Robert.

"Robert is from Paris,"

I tell Mrs. DeVine.

At home

we make a tent in the yard.

We pretend bears are outside.

We pretend to be terrified.

(That's a fancy word for scared.)

Then we play soccer.

We let my little sister play too.

Robert is a great kicker.

My dog runs around the yard.

"That's Frenchy," I tell Robert.

"She is not really French.

But you will like her anyway."

We go inside and

I show Robert my room.

"See? There's the Eiffel Tower,"

I say.

"Yes," says Robert.

"But that one does not

have a cowboy hat on it.

That Eiffel Tower is in Paris, France.

It is taller, and it is more famous.

But we have an Eiffel Tower too.

Our Eiffel Tower has a cowboy hat

on the top."

Wait a minute! I am very perplexed.
(That's a fancy word for mixed up.)
"But you're from Paris, France," I say.
"Aren't you?"

"No, I am from Texas.
Paris, Texas," Robert says.
"Ms. Glass told everybody
that the first day."
Robert shows me Paris, Texas,
on my globe.

Oh!

I guess I missed that part.

And I feel a little silly.

But not for long.

After all,

I have a new *ami*,

even if he isn't French.

Fancy Nancy's Fancy Words

These are the fancy words in this book:

Ami—"friend" in French (you say it like this: ah-mee)

Belle—"beautiful" in French (you say it like this: bell)

Bonjour—"hello" in French (you say it like this: bohn-joor)

Gorgeous—beautiful

Perplexed—mixed up

Tardy—late

Terrified—scared

I Can Read!

BEGINNING
1
READING

Fancy NANCY at the Museum

by Jane O'Connor

cover illustration by Robin Preiss Glasser

interior illustrations by Ted Enik

HARPER

An Imprint of HarperCollinsPublishers

For Susan Auerbach,
museum aficionada
—J.O'C.

For Sasha
—R.P.G.

To D.D.—bestest chum
—T.E.

Ooh la la!

I am overjoyed.

(That's a fancy word for very happy.)

Our class is going

to a museum.

I look extra fancy.
So does Ms. Glass.
"I love your shirt,"
I tell her.

Ms. Glass tells us,

"Today we will see masterpieces!

That's a fancy word

for great paintings."

The bus ride is very bumpy.

Bump! Bump! Bump!

Bree is my bus buddy.

"My tummy feels funny,"

she tells me.

Bump! Bump! Bump!

We stop for lunch.

Bree is not hungry.

But I am.

I eat my lunch.

I eat her lunch too.

I have two eggs,

a juice box,

carrot sticks,

an apple,

and a big cookie.

"*Merci*," I say.

(That's French for "thank you.")

Now we are back on the bus.

Bump! Bump! Bump!

"We will be there soon,"

says Ms. Glass.

I hope so.

My tummy feels funny now—

very funny.

Maybe two lunches was

one lunch too many.

"Ms. Glass! Ms. Glass!"
I cry.

"I am going to be sick."

"Stop the bus!"

Ms. Glass cries.

The bus stops.

Ms. Glass takes me

to the side of the road.

I get sick.

I drink some water.

I suck on a mint.

My tummy feels better.

But I am not overjoyed
anymore.

I am all dirty.

"I wanted to look extra fancy today,"
I say sadly.

"I understand," Ms. Glass says.

"And I have an idea."

We get to the museum.

"Come with me," says Ms. Glass.

I come out.

Ms. Glass's idea was spectacular.

(That's a fancy word for great.)

"Lucky you," says Bree.

"I wish I got to wear her shirt and hat."

"It is a French hat," I tell her.

"It is a beret."

A man from the museum

takes us to a gallery.

(That's a fancy museum word for room.)

I love all the paintings—
the masterpieces most of all.
We see paintings of trees and lakes.
They are called landscapes.

We see paintings of flowers
and bowls of fruit.
They are called still lifes.

The last painting is a picture of a lady.

"A painting of a person
is called a portrait,"
the man tells us.

"I like her hat and her fan and her beads,"
I tell the man.
"They are lavender.
Lavender is my favorite color."
(That's a fancy word for light purple.)

The man smiles.

"You are a very observant girl."

Then Ms. Glass tells us,

"Observant means noticing things.

Nancy is very observant, indeed."

On the bus trip back,

I do not feel sick.

I feel almost overjoyed.

That night,

I make a painting for Ms. Glass

because she is so nice.

Merci from
NANCY

It is not a masterpiece.

But someday I will paint one.

Fancy Nancy's Fancy Words

These are the fancy words in this book:

Beret—a cap (you say it like this: buh-REY)

Gallery—a room in a museum

Landscape—a painting of nature

Lavender—light purple

Masterpiece—a great painting

Merci—"thank you" in French (you say it like this: mair-SEE)

Observant—noticing things

Overjoyed—very happy

Portrait—a painting of a person

Spectacular—great

Still life—a painting of things such as flowers or fruit

I Can Read!

BEGINNING
1
READING

Fancy NANCY Sees Stars

by Jane O'Connor

cover illustration by Robin Preiss Glasser

interior illustrations by Ted Enik

HARPER

An Imprint of HarperCollinsPublishers

For stargazers everywhere
—J.O'C.

For Yarden and Yonatan,
who shine brightly in my heart
—R.P.G.

For the PA Stargazers,
whose friendship bends the Space/Time Continuum
—T.E.

Stars are so fascinating.

(That's a fancy word

for interesting.)

I love how they sparkle in the sky.

Tonight is our class trip.

Yes! It's a class trip at night!

We are going to the planetarium.

That is a museum

about stars and planets.

Ms. Glass tells us,

"The show starts at eight.

We will all meet there."

I smile at my friend Robert.

My parents are taking Robert and me.

Then Ms. Glass asks,
"What star is closest to Earth?"
That's easy.
It's the sun.

"What do you call stars
that make a picture?"
asks Ms. Glass.
Robert and Bree have both forgotten.
"I know, I know," I say.
"A constellation."

Ms. Glass nods.

On the wall are pictures.

There's the hunter and the crab

and the Big Dipper.

It looks like a big spoon.

We will see all of them at the show.

I can hardly wait.

At home, Robert and I

put glow-in-the-dark stickers

on our T-shirts.

Mine has the Big Dipper.

Robert has the hunter on his.

We spin my mobile

and watch the planets orbit the sun.

(Orbit is a fancy word.

It means to travel in a circle.)

Then we pretend to orbit

until we get dizzy.

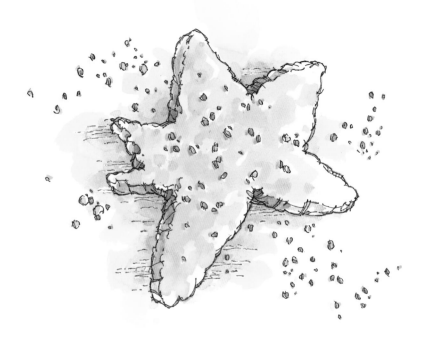

Later, we bake star cookies.

Sprinkles make them sparkle.

"The sun is a star,"

I tell my sister.

"It is the closest star,

so we see it in the day."

After dinner,

we wait for the baby-sitter.

She is very late.

Dad says not to worry.

We have plenty of time.

At last we get in the car.

Drip, drip, drip.

It is raining.

The rain comes down

harder and harder.

Dad drives slower and slower.

It is getting later and later.

A policeman comes over.

"The road is closed,"

he tells my parents.

"There is too much water."

Oh no!

There are cars in front of us.

There are cars behind us.

We are stuck!

"The show is starting soon!"

Robert says.

"We will not make it."

Drip, drip, drip goes the rain.

Drip, drip, drip go my tears.

Robert and I are so sad.

We do not even want any cookies.

At last the cars move

and the rain stops.

But it is too late.

The night sky show is over.

By the time we get home,

the sky is full of stars.

They are brilliant!

(That's a fancy word

for shiny and bright.)

I get a brilliant idea.

(Brilliant also means very smart.)

We can have

our own night sky show.

My parents get my sister.

We set up beach chairs.

Mom lights candles.

Dad puts the cookies on a tray.

We eat alfresco.

(That's fancy for eating outdoors.)

We watch the stars.

We see the North Star.

We see the Big Dipper.

All at once,

something zooms across the sky.

"A shooting star," Dad says.

"Make a wish!"

I tell Dad it is not a star.

It is a meteor.

But I make a wish anyway.

The next day Ms. Glass says,
"Everyone missed the show
because of the storm.
So we will go next week."
Everybody is very happy.
And guess what? My wish came true!

Fancy Nancy's Fancy Words

These are the fancy words in this book:

Alfresco—outside; eating outside is called eating alfresco

Brilliant—bright and shiny, or very, very smart

Constellation—a group of stars that make a picture

Fascinating—very interesting

Meteor—a piece of a comet that leaves a blazing streak as it travels across the sky (you say it like this: me-tee-or)

Orbit—to circle around something

Planetarium—a museum about stars and planets

I Can Read!

Fancy NANCY

The Dazzling Book Report

by Jane O'Connor

cover illustration by Robin Preiss Glasser

interior illustrations by Ted Enik

HARPER
An Imprint of HarperCollinsPublishers

For Owen Anastas,
a dazzling reader
—J.O'C.

For my dazzling *friend*
Sue Littman
—R.P.G.

For P.S., who saw the
potential joy contained
in a rainbow pack of
construction paper
—T.E.

Monday is my favorite day.

Why?

Monday is Library Day.

Before we leave, we select a book.

(Select is a fancy word for pick.)

It is like getting a present

for a week!

Bree selects a book on dinosaurs.

Robert selects a book

of funny poems.

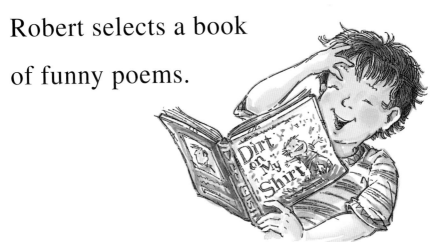

Teddy selects a scary story.

I select a book

about an Indian girl.

She has a fancy name,

Sacajawea.

You say it like this:

SACK-uh-jah-WAY-ah.

Later Ms. Glass has

thrilling news.

(Thrilling is even more exciting

than exciting.)

We get to do a book report!

"Your first book report.

How grown up!"

my mom says at dinner.

"Yes, I know," I say.

"My book is a biography.

It is about a real person."

After dinner I read my book.

Dad helps with the hard words.

I learn all about Sacajawea.

Sacajawea was a princess.

She lived two hundred years ago
out West.

She helped two explorers
reach the Pacific Ocean.

Mom takes me to the art store.

I need stuff for

the cover of my book report.

I want it to be great!

(I am the second-best artist

in our class.

This isn't bragging.

You can ask anybody.)

I get a bag of little beads,

some yarn,

and markers.

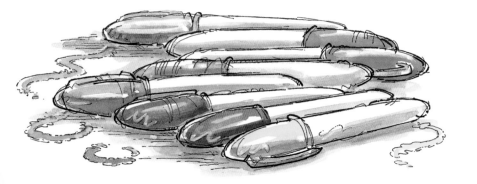

I start working on the cover.

I work on it every night.

I make Sacajawea look very brave,

because she was.

She found food for the explorers.

She kept them safe from enemies.

"Just remember to
leave time for the words,"
Mom keeps saying.
"I will. I will," I tell her.

"Ms. Glass wants you
to write about the book,"
Dad says over and over.
"That's what a report is."
"I know that!" I tell him.
Writing the words will be easy.

Ta-da! The cover is finished.

Sacajawea has yarn braids.

Beads and fringe are glued

on her clothes.

I must admit it is dazzling.

(That is fancy for eye-popping.)

Now I will write my report.

I get out lined paper

and a pen with a plume.

(That's a fancy word for feather.)

The trouble is, I am tired.

I know all about Sacajawea.

But the right words won't come.

What am I going to do?

I have to hand in my report tomorrow!

"I am desperate!" I tell Mom.

(That means I'm in trouble.)

Mom lets me stay up longer.

Still my report ends up

only two sentences long.

The next day,

everyone sees my cover

and says, "Wow!"

But hearing other reports
makes me nervous.
All of them are longer
than mine.
All of them are more interesting.

I read my report.

"Sacajawea was a heroine.

She helped people in trouble."

Everybody waits to hear more.

But there is no more.

I am crestfallen.

(That is fancy for sad and ashamed.)

"I spent too much time
on the cover,"
I tell Ms. Glass.

Ms. Glass understands.
"Why don't you tell the class
about your book?"

So I do.

I tell them all about

the brave things Sacajawea did.

Sacajawea was a heroine.

Ms. Glass is a heroine too.

At least, she is to me!

Fancy Nancy's Fancy Words

These are the fancy words in this book:

Biography—a story about a real person

Crestfallen—sad and ashamed

Dazzling—eye-popping, a knockout

Desperate—feeling trapped

Heroine—a girl or a woman who is brave and helps people

Plume—feather

Select—to pick

Thrilling—even more exciting than exciting

Fancy NANCY Pajama Day

by Jane O'Connor

cover illustration by Robin Preiss Glasser

interior pencils by Ted Enik

color by Carolyn Bracken

HARPER

An Imprint of HarperCollinsPublishers

For Mimi—a friend
forever
—R.P.G.

For A.B.: my long-sleeve
plaid flannel friend
—T.E.

"Class, don't forget!"

Ms. Glass says.

"Tomorrow is . . ."

"Pajama Day!" we shout in unison.

(That's a fancy word

for all together.)

I plan to wear my new nightgown.

I must say, it is very elegant!

(Elegant is a fancy word

for fancy.)

Then the phone rings.

It is Bree.

She says, "I am going to wear
my pajamas with pink hearts
and polka dots.

Do you want to wear yours?

We can be twins!"

"Ooh!" I say.

"Being twins would be fun."

Then I look at my elegant nightgown.

What a dilemma!

(That's a fancy word for problem.)

Finally I make up my mind.

I tell Bree I am going to wear

my brand-new nightgown.

Bree understands.

She is my best friend.

She knows how much

I love being fancy.

The next morning at school,
we can't stop laughing.
Everyone's in pajamas,
even the principal.
He is carrying a teddy bear.

Ms. Glass has on a long nightshirt
and fuzzy slippers.
I am the only one
in a fancy nightgown.
That makes me unique!
(You say it like this: you-NEEK.)

"Nancy, look!" says Bree.
"Clara has on the same
pajamas as me."

Bree and Clara giggle.

"We're twins!" says Clara.

"And we didn't even plan it."

At story hour, Ms. Glass

has us spread out our blankets.

She reads a bedtime story.

Clara and Bree lie
next to each other.
"We're twins,"
Clara keeps saying.

At recess

Clara takes Bree's hand.

They run to the monkey bars.

"Come on, Nancy," Bree calls.

But it is hard to climb in
a long nightgown.
And I can't hang upside down.
Everyone would see
my underpants!

At lunch

I sit with Bree and Clara.

They both have grape rolls

in their lunch boxes.

"Isn't that funny, Nancy?"

asks Clara.

"We even have the same dessert."

I do not reply.

(That's a fancy word for answer.)

Pajama Day is not turning out

to be much fun.

I wanted to be fancy and unique.

Instead I feel excluded.

(That's fancy for left out.)

The afternoon is no better.

Clara and Bree are partners

in folk dancing.

Robert steps on my hem.

Some of the lace trim

on my nightgown rips.

At last the bell rings.

I am glad Pajama Day is over.

"Do you want to come
play at my house?"
I ask Bree.

But Bree can't come.

She's going to Clara's house!

I know it's immature.

(That's fancy for babyish.)

But I almost start to cry.

Then, as we are leaving,

Bree and Clara rush over.

"Nancy, can you come play too?"

Clara asks.

"Yes!" I say.

"I just have to go home first

to change."

Now we are triplets!

Fancy Nancy's Fancy Words

These are the fancy words in this book:

Dilemma—a problem

Elegant—fancy

Excluded—left out

Immature—babyish

Reply—answer

Unique—one of a kind (you say it like this: you-NEEK)

Unison—all together

Fancy NANCY

The Show
Must
Go On

by Jane O'Connor

cover illustration by Robin Preiss Glasser

interior illustrations by Ted Enik

HARPER

An Imprint of HarperCollinsPublishers

*To Ethan Zarella and
Max Honig, my Power
Lunch pals
—J.O'C.*

*For my friends from the
Pennsylvania Ballet
—R.P.G.*

*For Script-Doctor L.B.:
This amazing Umpteenth
Act is all your doing
—T.E.*

"Quiet, please," says Ms. Glass.

"I have an announcement."

(That means she has something important to tell us.)

"The talent show is in a week."

Yay! Bree and I bump fists.

We have our act planned out already.

We will wear fancy circus costumes.

We will sing a song.

It is about daring girls on a trapeze.

Then Ms. Glass says,

"I am assigning partners."

Oh no!

That means we don't get to choose!

I am not assigned to Bree.

I am assigned to Lionel.

He is very shy.

I hardly know him.

Ms. Glass wants us

to brainstorm with our partner.

That means to talk over ideas.

So I ask Lionel,
"Do you like to sing?"
He says no.
He does not like to dance
or tell jokes.

He can wiggle his ears.

He can crack his fingers.

He can balance a spoon on his nose.

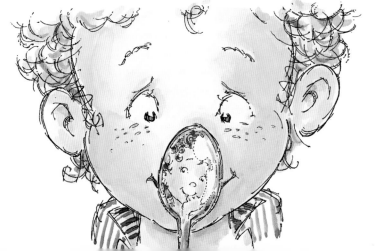

"Very cool," I say.

"But I can't do those things.

We need to perform together."

(Perform is a fancy word for act.)

That night I say,

"Bree and Yoko are partners.

They will do a fan dance

and wear kimonos."

(I explain that a kimono

is a fancy Japanese robe.)

"Lionel and I
can't think of anything to do."
I sigh a deep sigh.
"And now I won't get to wear
my circus costume."

Mom says, "Ask Lionel over.

Get to know each other.

It will help you plan an act."

On Saturday I ask Lionel over.

But his mom can't drop him off.

So Dad drives me to Lionel's house.

Ooh la la! It is very fancy.

It is almost a mansion.

Lionel's room is huge.

(Huge is much bigger than big.)

There are lots of toy lions.

"Oh! I get it!" I say.

"You like lions

because your name is Lionel."

I pick up a little glass lion.

"This is adorable," I say.

I tell him I like fancy words.

And adorable is fancy for cute.

Lionel shows me a lion mask.

"Wow," I say. "It's great!"

He puts on the mask.

"Grrr," Lionel says, and chases me.

We race all over his house.

"Help! Help!" I yell.

Later we have snacks.

"You're a great lion," I tell Lionel.

Then I get an extremely great idea!

"Let's do a circus act.

You can be the lion.

I can be the lion tamer.

I already have a costume."

Lionel likes the idea. Yay!

The next week we get together

many times to rehearse.

(That's a fancy word for practice.)

Still, we are nervous
on the day of the show.
We hear Ms. Glass announce,
"Here is Lady Lulubell
and the man-eating lion!"

The curtain opens.

Lionel jumps through the hoop.

Lionel walks on a pretend tightrope.

Then he roars and chases me.

"Don't eat me!" I cry.

"Eat this instead!"

I hand Lionel a huge lollipop.

He starts licking it and purring.

Then I curtsy and he bows.

Our act is over.

There is a lot of applause!

(That's a fancy word for clapping.)

I hear my dad shout, "Bravo!"

We all go out for ice cream.

I give Lionel a clay lion I made.

And guess what?

He teaches me

to balance a spoon on my nose!

Fancy Nancy's Fancy Words

These are the fancy words in this book:

Adorable—cute

Announcement—something important to tell

Applause—clapping

Assign—to choose something for someone else

Brainstorm—to talk over lots of ideas

Bravo—way to go!

Kimono—fancy Japanese robe

Mansion—a very fancy house

Perform—to act (or dance or sing)

Rehearse—to practice